ME TOO!

BY MERCER MAYER

A GOLDEN BOOK • NEW YORK

Western Publishing Company, Inc., Racine, Wisconsin 53404

Library of Congress Catalog Card Number: 82-84106 ISBN 0-307-11941-6/ISBN 0-307-61941-9 (lib. bdg.)
L M

When my little sister saw
me riding my skateboard,
she said…

Me too!

Then I had to help her ride.

I had a paper airplane
that I made myself.
But my little sister
saw it and said...

Then she threw it
in a tree.

I went hiking with my friends and my little sister said, "Me too!"

I had to carry her because she got tired.

When the snow fell I got my sled and went to the top of the hill.

Me too!

Guess what my little sister said.

I went skating on the pond.
My little sister said, "Me too!"
She doesn't know how to skate,
so I had to hold her up.

There was one last piece of cake.
My little sister said...

I had to cut it in half,
even though I saw it first.

When I went fishing
she said, "Me too!"
Then she caught
the biggest fish.

Everything I do
my little sister says,
"Me too!"

Today my little sister
had a candy cane of
her very own.

So I said…

Guess what my little sister said.